the fairly OddParents!

NICKELODEON

Timmy's
SCHOOL
SURVIVAL
Handbook

by Sarah Willson

SCHOLASTIC INC.

New York Toronto London Auckland Sydney
Mexico City New Delhi Hong Kong Buenos Aires

Butch Hartman

Based on the TV series *The Fairly OddParents*® created by
Butch Hartman as seen on Nickelodeon®.

ISBN 0-439-66667-8

12 11 10 9 8 7 6 5 4 3 2 1   4 5 6 7 8 9/0

Printed in the U.S.A.   40

First Scholastic printing, September 2004

Hi! I'm Timmy Turner, your average, ordinary ten-year-old.

And these are my fairy godparents, Wanda and Cosmo.

Cosmo: She's the smart one!

Wanda: He's ... well, he's cute, anyway.

Timmy: I'm going to give you the grand tour of my school . . . Dimmsdale Elementary. Do you go to school? If so, I'm sure you'll understand the kind of stuff I deal with. But having fairy godparents sure makes getting through the day a whole lot easier.

Timmy: All right, then! I wish I were invisible!

VANISH!

—"Cool!"

Cosmo: AAAH! Where's that voice coming from? Timmy's bedroom is haunted!

Wanda: It's Timmy, Cosmo. He's invisible.

Timmy: Wait! If I don't show up for class, it'll look suspicious. I need a fake Timmy to stand in for me.

ZAP!

Timmy: Aw, no one is going to believe that's really me, you guys. It looks totally fake!

FAKE TIMMY

Cosmo: Sure they will! It's two-dimensional! Just like you!

Wanda: Here's a remote. When you want the fake Timmy to say something, just press one of these buttons.

Sure! Okay! Whatever you say!

I'm not fake at all. I'm really Timmy.

Crash Nebula rocks, dude!

You look pretty in a dress!

Real Timmy: Well, having a fake Timmy might work, I guess. Let's see if my parents notice.

Fake Timmy: I'm not fake at all! I'm really Timmy.

Dad: Of course you're not fake. Well, bye, son! We'll wave as you get on the bus and ignore the fact that you're being pummeled within an inch of your life by the school bully!

Fake Timmy: Sure! Okay! Whatever you say!

Mom: Bye, Timmy, dear! Oh, and your father and I need some Us time, so Vicky will pick you up after school today!

Fake Timmy: *Sure! Okay! Whatever you say!*

Real Timmy: Wait! The clicker must be stuck! Vicky is the meanest baby-sitter on earth!

Cosmo: Well, look at the bright side . . . I found a nickel!

Wanda: Here comes the bus! We'll get the fake Timmy on board. You just make sure you get on the bus right behind him, Sweetie.

Cosmo: Hey! The fake Timmy keeps tripping. He's almost as clumsy as the real one!

Real Timmy: Welcome to my bus. I spend most of the ride trying not to get pummeled by Francis, the school bully.

Francis: Hey, Turner. I have someone I want you to meet:

MY FIST! AH-HA-HA-HA-HA!!!!

Real Timmy: The popular kids sit in the back.

Bodyguard: This area is reserved.

Real Timmy: Here comes Trixie! Hey! Maybe I'll have the fake Timmy say something to her, since I never get up the nerve.

Trixie: Hello, unpopular kids! Hello, Veronica, my fellow popular friend who is, however, not as popular as me.

Fake Timmy: *You look pretty in a dress!*

Trixie: Did someone say something?

Veronica: I didn't hear anything.

Real Timmy: Well, here we are at Dimmsdale Elementary. These are my best friends, Chester and A. J.

A. J.: I finished up the human genome project for extra credit last night.

Fake Timmy: Crash Nebula rocks, dude!

Chester: You are so right, dude!

Real Timmy: Hey! Being invisible is cool! I can do invisible stuff, like get back at Francis!

KICK ME

6

Real Timmy: Check this out. Now we're in Mr. Crocker's class. Besides the fact that he doles out Fs right and left, he definitely suspects that I have fairy godparents.

Mr. Crocker: Timmy Turner! This biology paper you wrote is far too accomplished for you to have written it yourself. There is only one explanation: You had help from your fairy godparents! So I'm giving it an **F- F** for the fairies who helped you!

Fake Timmy: You look pretty in a dress!

☆ **Real Timmy:** Wait! I didn't press any button!

Cosmo: Ooh. You're in big trouble now.

Wanda: Uh-oh. The clicker really is malfunctioning. Must be the batteries.

Mr. Crocker: The only way Turner could have seen me wearing that dress is with X-ray vision! That settles it! He *does* have fairy godparents! And I am going to find them with my secret heat-seeking fairy goggles!

Real Timmy: Oh, no. Mr. Crocker's going to detect my invisibility. I need a distraction! Quick! I wish there was a fire drill right now!

Real Timmy: That was close. Oh, great! Here comes Tootie! She's Vicky's little sister, and she's always trying to kiss me and stuff!

Mr. Crocker: Welcome back, class. Since there's just one minute left in this period, we have plenty of time for a pop quiz!

Cosmo: I bet I can fix the remote.

Wanda and Real Timmy: Noooo!!!

Fake Timmy: Sure! Okay! Whatever you say!

A. J.: Timmy wants to take a quiz? It must be a sign of the apocalypse!

Mr. Crocker: The real Turner would never say that. There is only one explanation: This must be an imposter, and the real Turner must be invisible! I will expose him and his fairy godparents once and for all!

MWAH-HA-HA-HA-HA!

Real Timmy: This is the cafeteria. The popular kids sit over there.

Where the popular kids sit

Real Timmy: And everyone else sits over there.

Where everyone else sits

Real Timmy: The most popular of the popular kids are Tad and Chad, the student body presidents. They get first-in-line privileges.

Trixie: Has anyone seen Timmy Turner?

Real Timmy: Trixie wants to talk to me! Quick! I wish I were visible!

POOF! APPEAR!

Trixie: Oh, there you are, Timmy Turner. I am doing a story about popularity for the school paper, and I need to interview a **total loser**. I may want to interview you later.

Real Timmy: Recess usually consists of me and my friends trying not to get pounded by Francis.

Luckily I am invisible today.

KICK ME

FRANCIS:

WHERE'S TURNER?

I BET HE DID THIS! WHEN I FIND HIM, I'M GOING TO KNOCK HIS BLOCK OFF AND THEN TEAR HIM IN HALF LIKE TISSUE PAPER!

Wanda: Isn't he mixing his metaphors?

Chester: Dude. You are so history.

Real Timmy: So now for the great unknown: the girls' bathroom! I can't believe I'm finally going to see what they do in there all the time!

...my: Welcome to gym class. This ...y not one of my favorite periods of the day . . .

Cosmo: Is that because you're really uncoordinated?

Real Timmy: Uh, a little more support here, please?

Wanda: Watch out for that ball, Sweetie.

Real Timmy: Uh-oh. Tootie. Good thing I'm invisible or she'd probably do something to really embarrass me. Let's take a look at what's in her locker.

the future Mrs. Tootie Turner!

TIMMY!
TIMMY!
TIMMY!

I Love ♡Timmy!

t + t =♡

true love forever!
TT
immy + Tootie
my TRUE LOVE!
Cosmo: Aww, I was just thinking her schoolgirl crush on you is really sweet . . . but now I think it's downright creepy!

Real Timmy: Well, it's the official end of the school day. But not for me–I mean, the fake me. Mr. Crocker gave the fake me detention, remember? As you can see, the place gets pretty deserted around here after the final bell rings.

Real Timmy: Uh-oh. I just remembered Vicky is supposed to pick me up after school today. She's going to kill me if she has to wait for me to finish detention.

Real Timmy: Hey! I'll just send the fake Timmy home with *her*, and I'll go to detention! I wish I weren't invisible any more!

POOF!

Mr. Crocker: Turner is walking right into my evil plot!

I know perfectly well that he is not the real Timmy Turner, but is a flimsily constructed duplicate fabricated by . . . his fairy godparents!

With this net I will capture the fake Turner and expose his ploy. Then I will finally be believed and will assume the reins of the New World Order!

MWAH-HA-HA-HA-HA-HA AAAAAAA!!

Real Timmy: Welcome to detention. For the next hour Mr. Crocker is going to grill me on the existence of fairies. But I'll never tell—never!

Wanda: Timmy! Watch out! There's a net right in front of the doorway!!!

Mr. Crocker:

I've got you now, Turner!

Real Timmy: Well, that concludes the tour of my school. Hey! I wonder what Vicky's doing with the fake Timmy right now.

Real Timmy: I'm glad you came along with me today. As you can see, school isn't always the greatest place when you're me-but I'm not complaining.

Having fairy godparents certainly makes it more interesting.
Only eight more years to go!
Right, guys?